Solomon and Mortimer

For William x

First published 2016 by Macmillan Children's Books
This edition published 2017 by Macmillan Children's Books
an imprint of Pan Macmillan
20 New Wharf Road, London N1 9RR
Associated companies throughout the world
www.panmacmillan.com

ISBN 978-1-5098-3045-9

1 3 5 7 9 8 6 4 2

A CIP catalogue record for this book is
available from the British Library.

Printed in China

Catherine Rayner

Solomon and Mortimer

Macmillan Children's Books

It's another calm day on
the banks of the river.

But it won't stay that way for long because...

Uh oh, here come two
bored little crocodiles.

It's Solomon and Mortimer,
and they're looking for some fun.

They've tried climbing trees,

which didn't go well.

And they've tried chasing lizards,

but the lizards weren't keen.

Flying looked fun,

but proved much too tricky.

So far, nothing had quite gone to plan.

So the bored little
crocodiles sulk down to
the river where the biggest
hippo is wallowing quietly.

Solomon smiles and thinks up a new plan.

"If we surprise him, he'll
make such a *big* splash!"

"The biggest hippo won't spy us here," Solomon whispers, as Mortimer quivers and grins.

But some passing pelicans shout from the air, "Solomon and Mortimer! What are you doing?"

"SHHHH!" hiss the crocodiles.

Hippo's ear wiggles.

Solomon and Mortimer
sneak nearer and nearer.

But some basking butterflies call suspiciously,
"Solomon and Mortimer, why are you hiding?"

"SHHHHHHHH!" they hiss.

Hippo's eye swivels.

Two cautious crocodiles creep closer than ever.

But an old toad croaks loudly, "Solomon!
Mortimer! You're up to no good!"

"SHHHHHHHHHHHHHHHHHH!"
they hiss.

Hippo's tail twitches,
ever so slightly.

Solomon and Mortimer are
perfectly positioned.

"What a big splash that hippo
will make," they chuckle naughtily.

They hold their breath,
their eyes tightly closed.

Squatting low in the water,
they are ready to leap.
When . . .

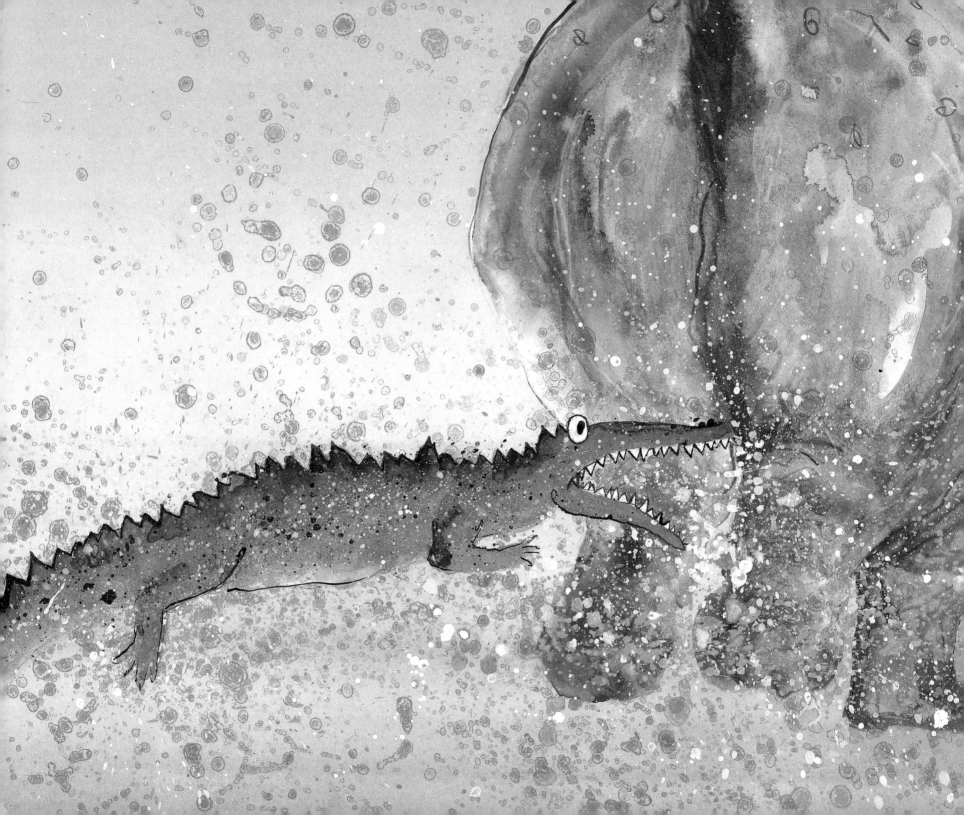

"BOO!"

shouts the hippo.

And
SPLASH
go the crocodiles!

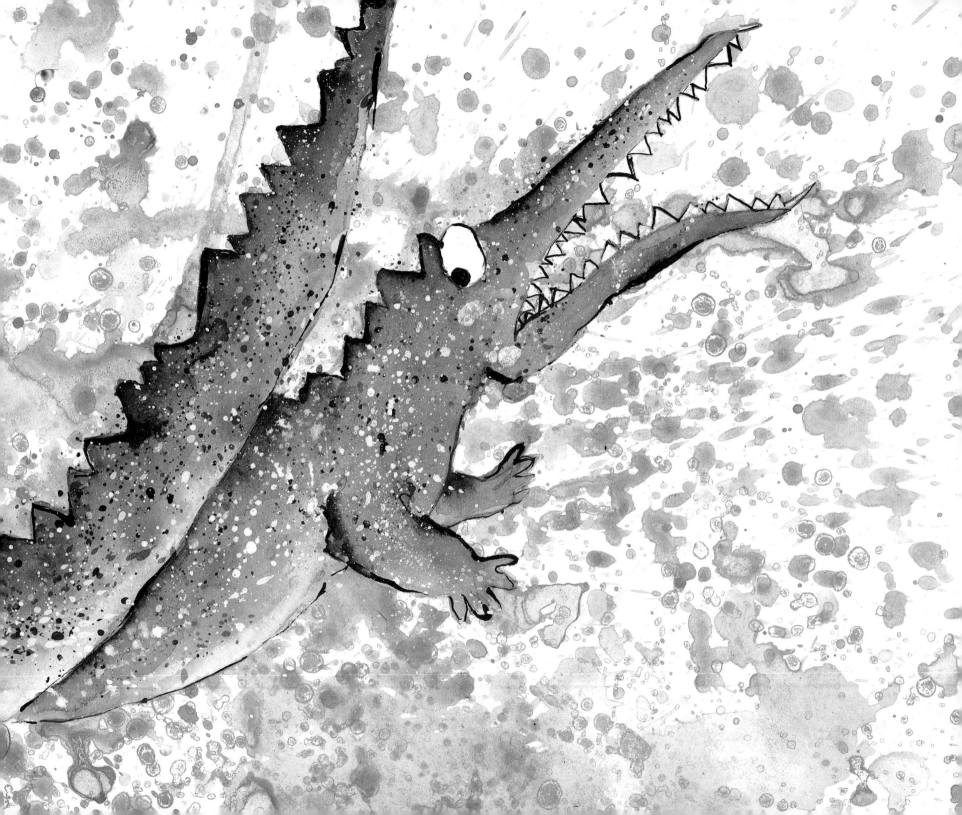

"Ha ha!" splutters Solomon.
"You made US jump!"
And everybody
giggles with glee.

"Who would have thought
that such a big splash came
from two little crocodiles..."